MARTYRDOM AND OTHER FREEDOM POEMS

PETER WUTEH VAKUNTA

iUniverse, Inc.
New York   Bloomington

MARTYRDOM AND OTHER FREEDOM POEMS

iUniverse books may be ordered through booksellers or by contacting:

iUniverse
1663 Liberty Drive
Bloomington, IN 47403
www.iuniverse.com
1-800-Authors (1-800-288-4677)

Because of the dynamic nature of the Internet, any Web addresses or links contained in this book may have changed since publication and may no longer be valid. The views expressed in this work are solely those of the author and do not necessarily reflect the views of the publisher, and the publisher hereby disclaims any responsibility for them.

ISBN: 978-1-4502-5141-9 (sc)
ISBN: 978-1-4502-5142-6 (ebook)

Printed in the United States of America

iUniverse rev. date: 8/20/2010

DEDICATION

In derision of all the cloned dictators in Africa

"It is clear that an African creative writer who tries to avoid the big social and political issues of contemporary Africa will end up being completely irrelevant like the absurd man in the proverb who leaves his house burning to pursue a rat fleeing from the flames" (Chinua Achebe, *Morning Yet on Creation Day*, 1975, p.78)

PREFACE

Martyrdom and Other Freedom Poems is the figment of the imagination of a malignant mind. We even suspect the poet to be some European nitwit who has had the chance to spend some time on African soil and misconstrued our existential modus operandi. A true son of the soil would never have the temerity to write down such balderdash about his homeland. We are dealing with a compulsive fraudster whose handiwork is nothing but a big hoax. Red blooded Africans will know how to unmask him and deride the half-truths contained in his book of poems, and have a good laugh at the implausibility of his insinuations. Nonetheless, if per chance some hoodlums should allow themselves to be hoodwinked by the sensationalism in this book, the malice harbored by this macabre poet, we count on our literary sages to raise a hue and cry against this wave of insanity; this flood of Afro-pessimism. We have half a mind to buy up all copies of this incendiary book from the publisher and burn them at the public square. But, doing so would amount to enriching in record time a wretch who actually deserves a dozen good lashes on his bare buttocks and a brief sojourn in one of our maximum security prisons. All things considered, the publication and sale of this book should be allowed for the sake of freedom of expression.

Table of Contents

I.
RAPE OF NATION-STATES

HICCUPS IN THE NEO-COLONY

Hic! Hic! Huc!
Hiccups of mental masturbation
Hic! Hic! Huc!
Hiccups of linguistic glottophagia
Hic! Hic! Huc!
Hiccups of cultural bastardization
Hic! Hic! Huc!
Hiccups of economic asphyxiation
Hic! Hic! Huc!
Hiccups of the Rape of Africa
Hic! Hic! Huc!
Hiccups of genocides
Hic! Hic! Huc!
Hiccups of denigration,
In all shapes and colors
Hic! Hic! Huc!
Hiccups of graft,
AND of wanton embezzlement
Hic! Hic! Huc!
Hiccups of ethnophobia
AND of misappropriation
Of public funds
Hic! Hic! Huc!
Hiccups of collusion
And of influence peddling
Hic! Hic! Huc!

Hiccups of the vicious circle of poverty
And of chronic underdevelopment
Hic! Hic! Huc!
Hiccups of endemic misgovernment
Hic! Hic! Huc!
Hiccups of Africanosomiasis
Hic! Hic! Huc!
Hic! Hic! Huc!
Of Mother Africa
iAfrica!
Hia!
The dawn of a New Deal
Hia!
The reign of meritocracy
The demise of jungle justice
Hia!
The requiem for nepotism
Hia!
The death of cronyism
Hia!
The inhumation of tribalism
Hia!
The cremation of chopbroke-*potism*[1]
Hia!
The entombment of spurious shibboleths
Hia!
The burial of shady deals
Of scratch-my-back
I-scratch-your-own credo,
Modus operandi of moral degenerates
How can these leaders liberate us
From mental slavery when they are
Actually begging for a re-colonization
Of their own countries?
Do I shock our leaders by telling them that

4

They are neo-slaves at the beck and call
Of their Western overlords?
Neo-overseers of the bleeding of their economies.
Do I shock my readers by pointing out
That these leaders are robbers, looters and mass murderers
When perpetrators of these anti-people crimes
Are announcing the fact on rooftops?

THE RABBLE

H-u-r-u-j-e!
Dawn of the UNITED STATES OF AFRICA!
H-u-r-u-j-e!
Muammar al-Gaddafi
H-u-r-u-j-e!
The foot soldier of African unity
H-u-r-u-j-e!
Warrior against Afro-pessimism
H-u-r-u-j-e!
Combatant against battered self-image
H-u-r-u-j-e!
Commandant of Africa's Salvation Army
H-u-r-u-j-e!
Africa must unite or perish
It boggles the mind
To think that we will
Salvage this continent by
Balkanizing it into ethnic concaves
Into tribal fiefs and war zones
This sort of tinkering spells doom
The future of Africa
    Rests on Africa's collective wisdom
    We cannot but unite
Behind one banner
To address our collective mishaps
African intelligentsia

Welcome a-board!
Gird your loins
H-u-r-u-j-e!
Sing Kum-Kum Massa
Oh! Kum-Kum!
H-u-r-u-j-e!
African youth
Oh! Kum-Kum!
The turn is yours
Oh! Kum-Kum!
H-u-r-u-j-e!
African women
Oh! Kum-Kum!
Big, big ngondere[2]
Oh! Kum-Kum!
Small, small ngondere[3]
Oh! Kum-Kum!
All hands on deck
Oh! Kum-Kum!
One time! GO! Africa! GO!
Pick up the flickering torch
Of Pan-Africanism
NO LOOKING BACK!
Forward ever,
Quip Ghanaian son of the soil.
United we stand
Divided we fall
The onus is ours
To rescue Africa
Rescue Mother Africa
From neo-colonization
i-Africa…
Not a continent for the taking
Not the lost continent
i-Africa…

Not the Dark Continent
Not a continent at risk
i-Africa…
Not a tabula rasa
Not a clean slate
i-Africa…
Has not reached
The proverbial point-
Of-no-return
i-Africa…
Is not irredeemable
Afro-pessimists
Despoilers of our backyard
May say what they want
They're like mosquitoes!
There's fire in the house
Run! Run! Run!
There's a storm in the palm-wine cup!
Run! Run! Run!
Le dehors est mauvais[4]
Up kontri done wuo-wuo[5]
Run! Run! Run!
There's hop-eye everywhere[6]
Run! Run! Run!
There's kelen kelen outside[7]
Run! Run! Run!
A sinister wind blows
Run! Run! Run!
Pandora's Box is open!
Run! Run! Run!
We call for a Sovereign National Conference
Sans objet![8]
We call for a Truth & Reconciliation Commission
No way!
Perpetrators squirming

Victims fuming
Toyi! Toyi![9]
Takes two to tango
BUT
A throng to toyi-toyi
Chant toyi toyi for fortification
Sing toyi toyi for glorification
The fallen heroes
Of Ntarikon
Sing toyi! toyi!
To the unsung heroines
Of Lake Nyos
Sing toyi! toyi!

RAZZMATAZZ

Statesmanship is one thing,
Politicking yet another
All too often the myopic
Muddle things up,
Perceiving self-service and leadership as bedfellows
It's but a fallacy?

The one adulates shibboleths and populism;
The other relishes selfless service
And heroic sacrifice
Abraham Lincoln, J.F. Kennedy
Nelson Mandela, Frederick de Klerk,
Patrice Lumumba, Kwame Nkrumah, Thomas Sankara, and ilk
Are poles apart from Verwoerd,
P.W. Botha, Jean Bedel Bokassa, Mbobutu Sese Seko,
Adi Amin Dadda, Adolph Hilter et al.

What's more?
The one gives it all;
The other takes it all,
Not even the crumbs
From their dining-tables reach the ground.
Worrisome dialectics you'd say!

UNSUNG HEROES

[This poem should be recited with background mournful music]
Legion are those compatriots/
Who paid the supreme price/
To safeguard our freedoms/
Yet, Nooremac[10] remains/
A hellhole where the rich feed muck to the poor/
In a sea of opulence/
Ruben Um Nyobé might have given up the ghost/
In the depths of the forest/
Of Sanaga Maritime/
Fighting for the liberation of Nooremacans/
Still, Nooremac remains a crab-house/
Where the fittest survive by undoing the feeble/
Ernest Ouandie might have been/
Eliminated on January 16, 1971/
In the name of Nooremacans/
Alas, Nooremac remains a Human Zoo/
Where predators prey on the wretched of the earth/
Bishop Albert Ndongmo might have/
Been arrested and convicted/
In December 1970/
Thanks to the machinations of Ahmadou Ahidjo[11]/
In the name of Nooremacans/
Too bad! /
Nooremac continues to stagnate in the doldrums/

Wambo le Courant/
Might have been a partner in "crime"/
With Albert Ndongmo/
For the sake of Nooremacans/
It's a pity! /
But Nooremac refuses to crawl/
Out of its perpetual claustrophobic lethargy/
Félix-Roland Moumié/
Nooremac's Marxist leader/
Might have been eliminated/
In Geneva by the SDECE/
(French Secret Service) with thalium/
Tant pis, Nooremac continues to be Golgotha /
Where miscreants and homicidal culprits call the shots/
Ndeh Ntumazah and Albert Womah Mukong/
Might have put their lives/
In jeopardy in the name of Nooremacans/
Alas, the wheel of national/
Deconstruction continues to grind/
And grind, and grind, and grind in perpetuity/
Slowly but surely toward abysmal disintegration/
Forget not Bate Besong alias BB! /
The Wonderful Man of Ako-Aya/
Obasinjom warrior/
National gadfly/
Whose penmanship is the cloth of our own nakedness/
His poetic Hosanna of Liberation/
More soothing than/
The spurious cacophonous choir/
Of the nation's grave-diggers—/
O Cameroon, Thou Cradle of our Fathers…/
Land of Promise, Land of Glory! /
Ha! Ha! Ha!! / (Laughter is therapeutic!)
Land of Promise, Land of Glory, my eyeballs! /
The Land is shaken to its very foundation/

By a polity in putrefaction! /
Decreed by the credo of *Chop-broke-potism*[12] /
By the creed of I-chop-you-chop-palaver-finish.../

RAINSTORMS

When did the rains
Start to beat us?
Was it when our country took
The wrong turn in Foumban?
When a people grope around in obscurity
Oblivious of whom they are
Not knowing where they're heading
Maybe that's because
They don't know
Where they hail from
And if they don't know
Their provenance
Then they've failed in the quest
For the fundamental self
Maybe that's because
They're out of touch with reality—
A rediscovery of the ordinary
Oftentimes,
We've been branded
Beasts of no nation[13]
The lost generation of Ambassonia
Aliens in the land of our birth
Some have christened
The children of this land
Fodder for military cannon,
Enemies in the house,

Maybe that's because
Myopia has bred conceit
In the convoluted minds
Of these nitwits
The future holds no good
For the jeune talent[14]
Of this blighted nation
Caught in political crossfire
And telltale demagoguery
Of egocentric djintété[15]
Swamped by the
Hullabaloo of lethal tribalism
And the brouhaha of ethnic cleansing
Swayed by the whirlwind
Of cronyism and cult worship
When the katika[16] do battle
The tchotchoro[17] of Ngola
Leak their gaping wounds
Smothering discontent
May lurk around like the nyamangoro[18]
But there comes a time
When even the mbutuku[19]
Picks up his boxing gloves
Like Mohamed Ali,
Like ear-munching Mike Tyson
And enters the box
To do battle with the foe
Till death do them part.

PARADISE OF IDIOTS

Basking in oxymoronic solace/
Of mediocrity, ineptitude and lethal myopia/
Self-styled 'People's Representatives'/
Metamorphosed numskulls/
Chatter like demented hoodlums/
In the abyss of the Glass House at Ngoa-Ekelle…/
Motion au Président de la République! /
Vive le Père de la Nation à la perpétuité! /
Long live Big Brother! /[20]
Handclapping semi-literates/
Kowtowing to the dictates of/
Diabolical machinations/
Orchestrated by an inept Executive/
Intoxicated by unbridled megalomania/
Enchained by the wheeling and dealing/
Of alien Machiavellian overlords/
Toying with the supreme law of the land/
Gerrymandering being the stock-in-trade /
Of this fawning band of demagogues/
These chameleons dance attendance/
On the threshold of the Palais d'Unité /
Den of occult pundits/
Macabre corridors of corrupt power/
That which corrupts absolutely/
To the chagrin of forgotten souls/
In the swamps of Elobi/
In far-flung backwoods of Donga Mantung/

At the expense of citoyens en détresse/
Chafing in makeshift shacks in Cassava Farms/
Hibernating in the dungeons of Kondengui/
And in those of New Bell and Mantoun/
Ours is a Tale of Woes/
From Solomon-the-Tortoise/
Through Lawrence-the-Sheep/
To incumbent Djibril-the-Chameleon/
The rubber-stamping continues unabated/
Warthogs and toothless bulldogs/
Sparrow hawks and castrated peacocks/
Dance macabre in the putrefaction of the Nation-State/
At the rhythm of the throbbing heart beat of Bamenda/
Suffocating in oversized strait-jackets/
Wherein they dare not budge/
Unable to see the limitations/
Of their own futile scheming/
And skewed prisms/
The possible advantages of an executive alternative/
Eludes these gawking-cum-fawning morons/
Accomplices in heinous crimes/
Of national Auctioneering/
Intoxicated by foams of inebriation/
Of foul play and influence peddling/
Adept in the art of cooking-the-books/
In the Paradise of Fowls/
Alias Parliament of Idiots[21]/
Take a walk down memory lane/
And speak of a momentous "event"/
And let's use quotation marks/
To serve as precaution/
What would that event be? /
The 1961 Foumban Plebiscite? /
The 1972 Peaceful Revolution? /
Or the 1982 Bloodless Waterloo? /

NATIONAL ANTHEM

Ma complice dem for Nkouloulou!
Ma tara dem for Moloko!
Ma mombo dem for Marché central!
Ma kombi dem for Kumba market!
Ma dong pipo dem for Kasala farm!
De wan dem for Camp Sic Bassa!
Ma complice dem for prison de Tchollire!
Da wan dem for 'Maximum security
Prison' for Mantoum!
Sef de wan dem for Kondengui.
I sei mek I langua wuna dis tori.
Some hymne national dung commot
Just now for Ongola.
Da mean say some national anthem
Dung show head for we own kontri.
Da anthem dem di sing'am sei:
Le Cameroun c'est le Cameroun,
That is to say,
Cameroon is Cameroon.
Da mean say,
Cameroon na Cameroon!

You wan pass for any Quat,
You di daso ya sei,
Le Cameroun c'est le Cameroun,
On va faire comment alors?

18

Da mean sei,
Cameroon na Cameroon,
We go na how-no?
Na so da Cameroon National Anthem dei!

Grand katika tif all moni
Go put'am for bank for Switzerland,
We di daso sing sei,
Cameroon na Cameroon,
We fit do na wheti sef?
Na so da Cameroon National Anthem dei!

Minister mof all nchou
For yi budget go put'am
For banda for yi long,
Antoine Ntsimi
Suivez mon regard!
We di daso sing sei,
Le Cameroun c'est le Cameroun,
Tu as déjà vu quoi?
Da mean sei:
You dong nye wheti sef?

Katika for CRTV
Bring yi kontri pipo come fullup
Office dem dei,
We di daso sing sei,
Cameroon na Cameroon,
Massa, we go do na how no?
Na so da Cameroon National Anthem dei!

Mange mille katch driver
For road take all yi nkap,
We go daso kop nye,
We di daso sing sei,

Bo, o garri dung pass wata-o!
Wheti we fit do no?
No bi na Cameroon dis?
Na so da Cameroon National Anthem dei!

Patron nyoxer[22] titi for yi planton[23]
For inside yi office,
Da woman yi massa go daso tok sei,
Ma broda, na dem get kontri,
You wan mek I do na how no?
Cameroon na Cameroon.
Na so da Cameroon National Anthem dei!
Gomna deny for put coal tar
For Ngoketunjia road bekoz
SDF dung gagner[24] election for dei,
Pipo go daso shake dem head,
Dem tok sei,
Kontri man, we go do na how eh?
No bi Cameroon na Cameroon?
Na so da Cameroon National Anthem dei!

Dem compresser[25] wok pipo
For Cameroon Marketing Board,
For CDC, or for Socapalm
Dem go daso wrap dem tail
For dem las like tif dog,
Tok sei: Papa God we go do na how-eh?
Cameroon na Cameroon.
Na so da Cameroon National Anthem dei!

Pikin commot for Ngoa[26]
Yi no get wok,
Yi papa wit yi mami
Go daso put dem hand for dem head,
Dem tok sei: you must go drive bendskin[27],

We go do na how?
Cameroon is Cameoon.
Na so da Cameroon National Anthem dei!

Grand Katika change constitution
Bekoz yi wan die for Etoudi,
Pipo go daso tok sei,
Frères on va faire comment alors?
Est-ce que les gens
De Bamenda vont accepter ça?
Le Cameroon c'est le Cameroun.
Na so da Cameroon National Anthem dei!

Mbere-khaki[28] shoot bendskinneur kill'am
Bekoz yi dung deny for tchoko[29],
Ala bindskinneur dem go daso,
Run go for inside matango club,
Begin cry sei,
Weh! Weh! Mon vieux,
Le dehors est mauvais,
On va faire même comment?
Le Cameroon c'est le Cameroun, non?
Na so da Cameroon National Anthem dei!

Chop Pipo Dem Moni party[30]
Tif election for Opposition,
Pipo dem go daso bend head
For grong dem cry sei:
Wah! Wah! Na how we go do-eh?
Cameroon na Cameroon
Na so da Cameroon National Anthem dei!

Grand katika,
Tif all moni for kontri go build hopita
For Baden-Baden for mukala kontri,

Camers[31] dem go daso knack hand, juah! juah!
Dem cry sei: God dei!
Some wan dem di tok daso sei:
Mon Dieu! Ne criez pas trop fort!
Le Cameroun c'est le Cameroun.
Na so da Cameroon National Anthem dei!

Le Père de la Nation,
Da mean say Father of the Nation,
That is to say Head of State,
Go carry ashawo come put'am
For Palais d'Etoudi,
Sei na First Lady,
Ongalais dem go soso knack mop sei:
Vraiment le cameroun est formidable,
Vivons seulement.
Da mean sei:
Cameroon na las,
Mek we begin nye daso.
C'est le comble!
Cameroon na Cameroon

Some okrika professor be see dis ting so,
Yi shake yi head two taim,
Yi sei: "This is the last straw
That broke the camel's back,
Cameroon dung capside!"
Na so da Cameroon National Anthem dei!

Ngomna for Renouveau
Dem cut pipo dem salary
Sef ten taim for one year,
Ma kontri pipo dem go daso
Run go for mimbo house,
Begin knack tori sei:

Massa, I never see dis kain
Wan before. Yi dung pass we.
Na which kain barlok dis-no?
Cameroon na Cameroon.
Na so da Cameroon National Anthem dei!
Clando ngomna tcha Lapiro de Mbanga
Président de tous les sauveteurs[32]
Go put'am for ngata,
Mek yi ton prisoner without no crime!
All ndinga pipo dem for Ngola
Dem go daso tok sei:
Çaaaa! On n'a jamais vu ça!
Mais on va faire comment alors?
No be Cameroon na Cameroon?

Yeye Katika for Ngola
Katch Joe la Conscience,
Alias Kameni Joe de Vinci
Go lock'am for Kondengui,
After yi send soja dem go meng
Yi pikin wei dem di call'am sei
Aya Kameni Patrick Lionel,
All 'freedom fighter' dem for Cameroon,
Dem go soso bend head for dem armpit,
Dem tok sei: upside dung wuowuo,
Any man fain road for yi long
Cameroon na Cameroon!

I dung ya dis ninga tok sotai,
I shake ma head.
I wanda for ma head sei, chei!
Dis Cameroon sef wei dem di tok so,
Yi dei na daso for dis grong,
Or na for ala planet?
I di wanda!

23

Na Bob Marley bi sing some yi own anthem sei:
'Liberate yourselves from mental slavery!'
I gring gi'am for Bob
Forseka sei mbutuku na ninga Number One!

II.
HOSANNAS OF LIBERATION

LONG AWAITED DAY

When the day
I've been waiting for shall arrive,
My tears shall dry up
Hate shall no longer swell in my chest
Nor jealousy in my eyes,
Love alone shall speak
The inaudible Language

When the day
I've been waiting for shall come,
Inequality shall be banished.
What shall remain will be
Distant memories of
Ten million aliens who
Counted for less than one million citizens
Five hundred natives;
Of millions of Africans
Deemed less important
Than a thousand whites.

When the day
I've been waiting for shall come,
The powerful will no longer
Dispossess the powerless of their land;
Nor rob them of the fruits of their labor.
No one will take advantage

Of the unwary anymore
Nor dupe the poor in spirit.

When the day
I've been waiting for shall come,
Injustice will no longer be the law of the land,
The jail will no longer be the abode of the innocent.
When the day
I've been waiting for shall come,
No one will turn his back to the beggar
In need of a slice of bread
Nor to those in dire need of a little warmth
Everyone shall extend a hand of friendship
To the universal neighbor

When the day
I've been waiting for shall come,
Homes will no longer be pillaged by bandits
Children killed for pecuniary reasons
Adolescents turned child soldiers
People will no longer lose their lives in meaningless wars
Waged in the name of so-called
Honor of nations

When the day
I've been waiting for shall come,
Peace will return to war-torn Africa
Equity will have a place
In Rapacious America
Slavery shall belong
In bygone times

And Coulies,
And Kaffirs
And Niggers

And Mau-Mau
And dirty black dogs
And the red war
And apartheid
Shall belong
In the self-same bygone times

Arrogant leaders,
Shall no longer wage wars
Based on differences in opinion:
Demented nations,
Shall return to sanity,
When the day shall come,
The day I've been waiting for.

TROUBADOUR

To write or not to write/
That is the question!
Fornicator of ideas/
Fumigator of illusions/
Of self-delusion/
Virtuoso of craftsmanship/
Heir of a nation in the pipeline/
ME, troubadour! /
I write poetry/
Therefore I am/
Herald of ill-wind/
That blows no one any good/
Purveyor of discomfiture/
To speak or not to speak/
Dilemma of the griot/
THE BARD…
Voice of the voiceless/
Loquacious Praise-singer /
Talkative zombie/
YOU…
Garrulous pen-pusher/
You create your own world/
A world of intoxication/
YOU… ME…TOWN CRIERS…
We create worlds/
Devoid of PREVARICATION/

Man and ilk are locked in/
Infectious mutual destruction/
Wife thinks husband is lying/
Husband believes wife is cheating/
Child thinks parent is fibbing/
Parent thinks child is faking/
Tax-collector believes/
Taxpayer is fawning/
Taxpayer thinks/
Tax-collector is feigning/
The politician thinks
The electorate is acting/
Voters think candidates
Are wheeling and dealing/
Pretty load of hogwash!
Garbed in multifaceted masks/
We make believe in all walks of life/
Foes act like friends/
Friends ape foes/
The world's theater for ape-manship/
Mortals impersonate immortals/
Humans pass for superhumans/
Miscreants act the pious/
Self-seekers masquerade/
As selfless philanthropists/
The world is like a mask/
He that desires to see well/
Dare not stand in one spot/
The Muses said this would happen:
That language would be hijacked/
And words will be twisted out of signification/
By a couple of tricksters/
From the Tower of Double-Speak/
And from then verbal merchants/
Will live in an infernal Tower of Babel/

Words would get crooked/
And more and more crooked/
As meaning will be butchered out of signification/
On the altar of linguistic jugglery/
No one would understand/
What the other is saying/
Or to look at the mouth/
Of his neighbor/
When it is best to shut up/
We live in that time/
That the Sage had predicted/
Nothing means what is said/
What is said is not what is meant/
And what is done is not what is expected/
Words say what they don't mean to say/
In our pseudo-lingo/
SLANGUAGE...

MARTYRDOM

[The reading of this poem should be accompanied by barely audible sobbing]

Their bodies lie rotting
In mass graves all over the land!
Their ghosts ignited
Les villes *mortes,*
Infamous ghost-town operations,
Civil disobedience movement,
Last ditch battle with vampire politicians
That brought life
To a virtual standstill
In Mimboland—
Taximen,
Bayam-sellam,[33]
Bendskin drivers,
Sauveteurs,
Pousse-pousseurs[34],
Unsung heroes of No Man's Land
Doggedly refused to throw in the towel,
Man no die, man no rotten!
They chanted.
The Takembeng[35]
Symbol of feminine stoicism,
Joined the processional dirge,
Baying for the blood of knock-kneed Mbivodo!

Bereaved families consulted
Maguida[36] for gris-gris,[37]
Many more went to seek occult fortification
From the mami-wata[38]
Aquatic inhabitants of
Lake Oku,
Lake Manenguba,
Lake Nyos,
And,
Sanaga River,
To what intent?
Smoke shriek-voiced Mbiya Mbivodo
And his Ali Baba Gang
Out of the Shit House at Etoudi,
Den of compulsive chop-broke-potters!
Hell-bent on crippling the nation
Via necromancy and megalomania
Through kleptomanic gerrymandering.
In Abakwa,
The downtrodden chanted:
Mbiya is really up to something!
He must go!
Facing Mount Cameroon,
Chariot of the gods,
The wretched of the earth roared:
Red card for Mbiya Mbivodo!
In Bafoussam and Bafang,
In Loum Chantiers Gare,
In Penja and Dibombari,
In Nkongsamba and Kake,
Insensed rioters sang freedoms songs:
Liberté eh, eh!
Liberté eh eh eh eh !
Dieu tout puissant ah ah!!
Nous serons libres bientôt!

In Nkambe and Wum,
In Bamunka and Babessi,
In Bamali and Babungo,
In Bambili and Bambui,
In Bali and Babanki,
In Kumba and Kumbo,
Disillusioned protesters chorused:
Liberty, oh, oh!
Liberty oh, oh, oh, oh!
All-powerful God, ah ah!
Soon we'll be free!
But the Man,
Being no spring chicken
Smelling arata,[39]
He sneaked incognito
Into the equatorial forest
To obtain from his pygmy tribesmen
Megan[40] which he carries on his body
Day in day out,
At night and in broad daylight,
In bed and out of bed,
As backup for his European-tailored
Bullet-proof jacket,
In his peregrinations
Through the ghost nation he claims to govern.
GHOST TOWNS OPERATIONS...
Towns haunted by ghosts of victims,
The ghost of Eric Takou,
Phantoms of freedom fighters,
Cut down by bullets fired by
Trigger-happy semi-literate
Soldiers and gendarmes[41]
Apparitions haunt this defiled land in perpetuity.
The brutal killing of innocent kids
Shocked women who exposed their cunts

To the blood-thirsty killers of their offspring,
Protesting the murder of innocent victims
The corpse of Takou,
Paraded in a pousse-pousse[42]
By irate inhabitants of Douala
Deposited at the doorstep of his assassin
VENDETTA!

RAMADAN

I took part in the fasting,
I took part in Ramadan.
Ramadan is over,
The month of self-imposed fasting has come to an end.
When shall involuntary fasting
Come to an end in this land of plenty?
Fasting willy-nilly by the indigent families in dire need?

I took part in the fasting.
With my Moslem friends;
I drank no water,
I ate nothing during the day.
My body withstood the pangs of hunger,
But my soul, Lord,
Is not saved!

This afternoon, as I ate my first meal of the day!
This evening as I sat down at table,
Did I feel myself closer to the world's starving populations?
Those souls
Underneath the white boubous
Donned by those celebrating the feast of Ramadan,
Are they saved?
At the public square
Where white gandouras
Squatted in festive mood,

I saw several empty spaces:
Places reserved for those who shall
Never witness the end of Ramadan.

III.
STREAM OF
CONSCIOUSNESS

THE MAVERICK

From grass to grace
By dint of hard work
From indigence to opulence
By the sweat of your brow
From shack to White Palace
Through selfless service

To all and sundry
From inner city to suburbs
By the pull of your own bootstraps
Hail Barack, Uncle Sam's Maverick!
Unfazed by the macabre cacophony of detractors
You forged on à l'instar d'un guerrier africain.

Hail Hussein, Miracle Performer
L'enfant terrible in the land of the brave!
Unperturbed by litanies of doomsayers
You trudged on, oblivious of taunts from adversaries—
Shame on you… You lie… et patati patata
Victory you set your eyes on.

The summit you focused your gaze on
Vous êtes arrivé au poil,
Salut à vous, Président Obama!
Le peuple vous salue et vous rend hommage
Qui aurait cru? Qui aurait osé rêver?

Néanmoins, vous voilà donc à la Maison Blanche!

Do you remember that day?
How could you forget Historic November 4 2008?
On that day B.H.O. took the world by storm!
On that day the scales fell of our eyes
And we stopped perceiving the world
Through rose-colored glasses.

On that day B.H.O. chanted: YES WE CAN!
Tom, Dick and Harry chorused: YES WE CAN!
I said to doubting Thomases: NEVER SAY NEVER!
To crown glory with glory
Norwegian August Body
Yet another red feather to your cap is affixed —

Nobel Prize for Peace!
In this Hall of Fame
You rub shoulders with Baobabs
Like Martin Luther King, Mother Theresa
Nelson Mandela and ilk.

SECOND TO NONE

Under your fingers
My translucent body quaked
And quivered even more
When your lips touched mine
Suddenly, the world
Became sweet like honey
Your hand on my breast
And your head on my shoulder
Transformed my erstwhile
Grief into nondescript joy;
How much shall I give you
In return for this singular experience?
"O time, halt your flight!"
Let me hear the beating of your heart
Lest my broken heart
Concealed by my silk dress
Begin to fathom mirages.
Your hand on my breast
And your head on my shoulder
How much shall I pay you
For this unique experience?

GREAT WORDS

There are great words in our language.
One such word is "Thanks."
There are weighty words in our lingo
Two such words are "Forgive me."

There are mighty words in our slang.
Three of such words are "I love you."
Take time to internalize these words
They work like magic!

TIME

Take time to express gratitude
Whenever someone does you a good turn,
One good turn deserves another.
To give thanks is the norm!

Take time to ask for forgiveness,
Whenever you err
To err is human.
And forgiveness is divine.

Take time to love,
Love is a pearl
Unconditional love begets happiness.
God is Love.

As it were,
Time and tide wait for no one
But time and tide usher in change
To the chagrin of all and sundry

So it transpires
That yesterday's oppressors
May come full circle
And metamorphose into today's liberators.

Time is a great healer
So it will happen that
The underdogs of today
Will become the overlords of tomorrow.

BETTER HALF

[Tribute to my wife]
Apple of my eye
You surpass all epithets
You aren't superhuman
Yet you've carved a niche
Deep down in my heart of hearts

Your deep sense of integrity
Overshadows petty flaws
You aren't a paragon of virtues
Yet you exude confidence
And inspire true love

Icon of feminine stoicism
Beacon of hope for Womanhood
These words, my love
A Hosanna of love
Homage to my tower of sterling qualities.

TRIBUTE TO A MENTOR!

Farfesa[43] Ladi,
Soon you'll say to UW Campus,
Sai wani lokaci!
Sai mun hadu!
We'll miss you!
You'll no longer be here.
Yet your sterling legacy lives on!

Professor Linda Hunter.
Before long you'll say to Van Hise,
Au revoir[44]!
We'll miss you!
You'll be far and away
But the lantern you've
Kindled shines on!

Malama[45] Ladi,
In a short while you'll say to Bascom Hill,
So long!
See you later!
We'll miss you!
Nevertheless, the seeds you've
Planted will germinate to fruition.

Farfesa Hunter
We all say:
Mun gode!
Thanks!
Ndoh loh!
Merci!
Gracias!

BARREL OF THE PEN

A bazooka shoots to kill;
My pen scripts to annihilate.
Like a bulldozer it levels all
Minutiae in its path—

Graft, perversion, ineptitude,
Corruption, nepotism, cronyism,
Adultery, bigotry, racism, sexism,
Gravy train and much more.

Cannons boom to exterminate;
My pen scribbles to kill.
No one goes unscathed.
It has scores to settle with all and sundry.

A missile detonates hitting
Objects in its orbit.
My pen blasts to lambaste butts
Right, left, and center.

It's no respecter of social status.
Nor tribal affiliations
It doesn't revere caste.
It's the voice of the voiceless.

POETRY

Bard, I am
I write verse therefore I am.
Poetry is not dead wood
As many would have it.
Verse is a vehicle for the
Transportation of mixed emotions—
Some sweet, others bitter.

Griot, I am
Poets create their own world;
A world as it should be,
Devoid of cobwebs,
Bereft of prejudice,
Poetry stands for a worldview,
Crucible of creative imagination.

Poet, I am
Poetry performs a myriad functions—
How reverent the lyrics of our Anthems!
Isn't that poetry?
How soul-searching the melody of our hymnals!
Isn't that poetry too?
How captivating our rhymed adverts!

Pas un pas sans bata!
That too is poetry!
Praise-singer, I am
Poetry is not dead wood.
It's a showcase of verbal artistry,
A genre in its own right,
Vive la poésie!

SUMMUM BONUM

In keeping with the tenets of the social contract,
The good of one is the good of all and sundry.
It's no good living on an
Island like a hermit.
The more the merrier.

The good of the individual
Is the common good.
Man is worthy only in
The presence of others.
No Man is an island

Seek ye not the Self;
Seek rather the Other,
Recipe for boundless LOVE.
The common good bears
Seeds of universal peace.

STOP LIGHTS

In this fast train
Where we are:
Teenagers falling pregnant,
We need stop lights to halt the insanity.

In this top-speed train
Where we are:
Underage kids wielding firearms,
We need red lights to stop the lunacy.

In this breakneck train
Where we are:
School kids peddling hard drugs,
We need red lights to halt the dementia.

In this maddening train
Where we are:
Minors consuming liquor with no qualms,
We need stop lights to stop the madness.

In this high-speed train
Where we are:
Young mothers tossing newborns into dumpsters,
We need stop lights to halt the derangement.

THIRD EYE

Watch yourself go by day in day out.
Perceive yourself as "S/he", not "I".
Find fault with yourself as you'd with others.
Confront yourself unabashedly every moment.

Watch yourself go by each day.
Read meaning into your every action and intention,
As you would do unto others.
Let unmitigated criticism surge through you.

Watch yourself go by each day.
Reproach yourself for every flaw.
Without taking the log out of your eyes,
Attempt to see the speck in the eyes of others.

Watch yourself go by each day.
Stand by and watch yourself with a third eye.
If you'd muster the courage do this,
It would dawn on you that you

Lack the moral high ground on
Which to stand and judge others.
Your love for all and sundry will grow like
Mushrooms on a decaying tree.

FETTERED INTERCOURSE

War or Peace?
That is the question!
Just or Unjust war?
Your answer is as good as mine.

The spectacle of our men and women
In khaki armed to the teeth with weapons of mass
Destruction acting unilaterally
To invade a lesser nation,

Purportedly to destroy weapons of mass destruction
Deeply violates the notion of rationality.
The chief threat to
Global peace today

Seems to be US not THEM.
The logic of preemptive war
Clearly is inimical to common sense.
A safe nation is not one that glorifies militarization

Rather the one that cherishes peaceful resolution of conflicts
A nation that does not respect life
Harbors the germs of its own annihilation.
An attack on perceived enemies beats logic

The disgraceful comportment of our men
And women in uniform at Abu Ghraib
Has opened a Pandora's Box,
That sets loose macabre demons of self-destruction.

QUIET PEACEMAKERS

I have half a mind to
Turn and live with the DOVES.
They are forever tranquil.
I watch them in utter admiration.

They do not whine and pine
About the graft and grime of society,
They are not anxious about what tomorrow
Has in store for them.

I have half a mind to
Turn and live with the DOVES.
They don't anger me with tales of lust,
Except when they are in season.

None pats me on the back for dereliction of duty.
I have half a mind to
Turn and live with the DOVES.
None amasses wealth to the chagrin of others.

I have half a mind to
Turn and live with the DOVES.
None abuses power.
No one exploits the other unashamedly.

I have half a mind to
Turn and live with the DOVES.
None indulges in debauchery.
Not a single one harbors lurid desires.

I have half a mind to
Turn and live with the DOVES.
No one builds castles in the air.
They all accept their lot in life.

COLORED PEOPLE'S TIME

It beggars belief that at this time and age
Quite a few folks continue to cling unto the
Concept of 'Colored People's Time'.
Against all logic!

Oftentimes, I hide my face in utter shame as
I watch my brethren walk leisurely into a
Board room to attend a meeting that
Began hours ago!

'Colored People's Time' stems from a primitive
Mindset that restricts us to reading time
By observing our shadows, movement of
The sun and moon, and listening to the rooster.
'Colored People's Time' confines us to counting
Rivers, brooks and hillocks in order to measure distances
Between our towns and cities,
This defies common sense!

Decency dictates that we be punctual at all times.
Punctuality is a hallmark of the civilized.
It is bears testimony to our respect
For other people's time.

NO MAN'S LAND

You call me makwerekwere[46],
You brand me sans papiers[47]
But who are you?
Sanctimonious hypocrite!

This land is
No man's land!
You swiped it from Natives,
This land is No man's land!

It is land of the aborigines
This land belongs to no one—
It belongs to everyone—
You, me, he, she, they...

This land is no man's land!
All and sundry came here
From other climes
Fleeing persecution at home!

It's an irony of sorts,
Though, that some inhabitants of this land
Are relegated to second-class citizen status on
Account of provenance and race.

This land is no man's land!
Bigotry governs this land!
Ignorance is a canker eating deep
Into the fabric of this land!

This land is No man's land!
Those who arrogate
To themselves the label 'autochthons'
Know nothing about their history.

This land is No man's land!
Know your history!
Pigheaded morons!
Ignorance is not bliss!

OTHER VISTAS

To live in isolation
Not caring a fig about what's transpiring around
May be a harbinger of doom.

Ignorance of other horizons may be lethal.
Think of the devastating wars fought
Since the dawn of history—

Root cause is bigotry.
Bigotry breeds prejudice;
Prejudice engenders belligerence

Bellicosity gives birth to violence.
History is replete with glaring examples.
Think of the holocaust—

Genocide of millions of
Jews in Nazi gas chambers!
Think of the Rwandan genocide.

Remember the Persian Gulf War.
Recall the Ethiopia-Eritrean feud.
Don't forget the Libya-Chadian War.

Ponder the Cold War.
Think of operation Iraqi Freedom

Consider Slobodan's massacres in Bosnia.

Poom Pang! Boom Bang!
Poom Pang! Boom Bang!
Poom Pang! Boom Bang!

Sometimes all it takes to avert a full-scale
War is to crawl out of one's self-imposed cocoon
And embrace other vistas.

We can't build global peace
By vegetating in our little holes in perpetuity
To broaden one's horizons is to cultivate the global garden.

IV.
WHEN YOU'RE YOUR WORST ENEMY

FIFTH COMMANDMENT

Once upon a time,
There lived a sagacious man
Who had toiled year in year out
To raise his sons the best way possible

One day the ubiquitous thief came
And stole the man's heart —
The man died.
Much to the chagrin of his sons.

Strong in their belief
That the dead are not dead,
Better still,
The dead watch over the living

The sons decided to cater
To the well-being of their deceased,
In Nihamboloho—land of the dead
By giving him some pocket money.

While the man lay in state,
The first son approached the casket,
Pulled out $500 bills,
Placed them beside his dad and said:
Pa, take this and spend it on your
Way to Nihamboloho—

Then came the turn of the second son,
Not wanting to be outsmarted by his siblings

He pulled out $1000 bills,
Placed them in the casket and said:
Pa, take this pocket money and use it
On your journey to Nihamboloho

And then it was the turn of the youngest son
He walked up to the casket,
Took the $1500 bills lying there,
And put them into shirt pocket

Then he took out a checkbook from his pocket
Weeping abundantly,
He wrote a check for $1500,
Dropped it in the casket and said:

Pa, I am very concerned about your security in Nihamboloho,
Armed robbers may mug you on the way,
They may even kill you for your money!
Take this check and spend it as you travel to Nihamboloho.

PSEUDO-INTELLECTUALS

Ponder this irony of sorts!
An impressive number of self-styled
Academics in our midst are pseudo-intellectuals
Counterfeit academics

Highly qualified but unschooled!
Nomenclature for these fraudsters is extensive—
Okrika professors, kokobioko professors, kubakuba professors
Paycheck professors, professors without publications...

How can one flaunt a bagful
Of degrees and yet comport oneself
In the most uncouth manner possible,
Like a motor-boy at the taxi rank?

Pseudo-intellectuals are blokes
Who have been to college
Yet no college has gone through them!
Quack intellectuals!

Conventional wisdom ordains
That a learned mind be couth at all times.
To be educated is not synonymous with qualification
The educated are refined in garb and deed

The schooled mind is a role model in word and deed.
Anything short of that is tantamount
To pulling wool over the eyes of people,
Away with pseudo-intellectuals!

BULIMIA NERVOSA

I have a maddening craving for food.
I long for junk food.
I eat like a horse:
At home, at work, in my car, everywhere!
Alas, this craving for food is taking a harsh toll on me.
Is it a bane or a boon!
My physique speaks volumes—

I am a roving mountain.
I have grown a second belly
My cheeks sag,
My elephantine legs too heavy to move!
My legs as heavy as lead.
I suffer from insatiable hunger,
Yet I throw up after each meal!

I gasp for breath.
I am ill at ease!
I am on the horns of a dilemma—
To eat or not to eat?
I abhor obesity
And yet I dread anorexia.
I am in the throes of a bulimic dilemma.

FATE

Love's various phases,
Disappointments, sins and breakups
Come in rapid succession,
As heavy as the kiln
This is my fate--
The most painful experience
Often the inevitable breakup:
Break with Love
Break with the past
Break with the present
Break with the one's faith
Break with promises
Break with ecstasy
And contemplation of the future
With only one hope in mind!
You know only too well
That this life-style is out of tune with me
                    There,
I searched for peace in vain.
                    Here,
I suffered many times
And in all this
You've not shown me where I belong
You know you made me a sensitive being
I feel pain deeply and interminably.
You know full well that

I am in despair, total hopelessness.
                    Yet
You've not set me free.
You're waiting for me to make the decision
                    To kill myself
And then you'd punish me
                    For suicide
So that even in your kingdom
I'd have no place.
Am I heretic?
Or agnostic?

NOOSE

The root cause of pathos in this day time and age
Is insatiable materialistic craving…
The belief that materialism begets bliss,
Getting all that we want does not vouchsafe happiness.
Truth of the matter…
Our desires are our own undoing.

Sure route to bliss?
Quest for things immaterial…
Possessions that inspire genuine happiness,
If we plant our hearts
Solely in material possessions,
End result would be catastrophic.

Oxymoronic as it may sound,
More often than not,
Things desired are seldom valued.
Choose and let live,
Solomon's wisdom,
Steer clear from putting your head in the noose.

MANACLES

Man born free, man born fettered.
In chains everywhere--
Fetters of daily toil;
Chains of substance abuse;
Shackles of social upheavals;
Chains of moral decadence;
Manacles of matrimonial infidelity;
Chains of cerebral servitude;
Bonds of fundamentalist bigotry;
Chains of imperialist yoke,
Manacles of rivalry
Man entangled in
Shackles of bondage!
Mankind hard at
Work decimating womankind.
Womenfolk engrossed in the
Task of undoing men!
Each passing day portends
Woe for humanity's predicament.

KID POWER

[This poem is dedicated to teenagers]

As far as parental duty goes,
You have misplaced priorities,
Children First!

What's this phrase?
Didn't I hear that?
What does it mean?

Kids should rule our lives?
Kids' rights without responsibilities?
Kids' free rides through life!

Freedom! Freedom!
Word often abused.
Teenagers! Teenagers!

Cancerous new buzz word that gives
Leeway to misdemeanor!
Freedom is seldom synonymous with recklessness.

GODS OF STEEL

How many times
Shall this lofty scene
Be enacted over and over?

I flex my muscles,
I prime my gun;
I pull the trigger, poom! poom!

My foe drops dead
In a pool of blood,
Does that solve my problem?

He that cherishes peace;
Prepares for war,
There goes the old wives' tale again!

Humankind is deranged!
Very sick, indeed,
Do I have to annihilate in order to build?

That's the modus operandi
Of Gods of steel
Of belligerent nation-states.

I listen to the voice of reason screaming
Peace! Peace! Peace!
War-mongering noting but bravado in futility.

PREDATORS

Predators leap after preys,
Hunter becomes the hunted.
That man is his own worst enemy.
Take a walk down memory lane.
Revisit the Jewish holocaust.
Have a flashback on Hiroshima
Recall Verwoerdian South Africa;
Bastion of sanctimonious hypocrisy
And racial cleansing,
Ponder the harrowing bloodbath
Perpetrated by Hutus and Tutsis in Rwanda,
Think of Neo-Nazism the world over.
Revisit the nightmarish massacre of
September 11 in America and its aftermath,
These melancholy events bear testimony
To man's bestiality!

DOGS OF WAR

He that seeks peace,
Prepares for war,
An armed nation is a safe nation.
Fatalistic Fallacies!
Take these admonitions
With a pinch of salt,
Those who declare war seldom know
They will perish in war.

The mayhem wrecked
By gun-toting child soldiers,
Bears testimony to the rape of childhood,
School premises converted to war zones!
The craze for firearms,
Trigger-happy delinquents,
In every nook and cranny,
The specter of death

Hangs over our heads
Like the sword of Macbeth.
The media has further
Emboldened us by churning out the hollow
Propaganda that a gun-free
Nation's a safe nation.
Scoff it!
Tall tale!

MAKE OR MAR

This is but a fact of life,
Greatest pleasure in
Living is that one good turn
Deserves another.

In this fast-paced world,
It's easy to be so engrossed
In oneself that one forgets to
Lend a helping hand when need be.

The essence of life is not
To stand for everything there is.
 Rather, it's to stand for something
 That makes a difference in life.

Perforce, we're in this together.
By this token,
Makes sense to gun for
The Common Good.

GREEN HORNS

This asteroid of ours
Is replete with myriads of vendors,
But the mother of them all
Are merchants of gray matter.

The nomenclature is legion—
Instructors, teachers, professors,
Evangelists, pastors, priests,
Ad infinitum.

All aboard the ship
Of intellectual spoon-feeding
The noble task of
Molding young minds for seminal tasks.

Whether you be teachers,
Principals, professors or ministers,
The prime duty is onerous,
Nurture green minds.

Need dictates that we
Learn or perish.
The ability to learn from
The cradle to the grave,

Sets humanity apart
From other forms of life
How come we tolerate
Charlatans in academia?

BAOBABS

Size not Might.
The white ant is
Pretty minuscule,
Yet in less than no time
It would demolish a baobab.

Little nations
Like big nations engender the Global Village.
There aren't lesser nations,
Each one has a vital role to play.
In the crucible of universalism.

Fair play or foul?
Do unto others
What you would
Have them do unto you.
Not the other way round

No nation has
Monopoly over warfare.
Pacifists of today
May be war-mongers of tomorrow.
Nation that has been bitten by snakes fears millipedes.

The terrorists of today may become
The peacemakers of tomorrow,
We're all vulnerable to vagaries of life.
It has happened elsewhere;
It can happen here.

COCK- AND- BULL

Man and man are locked
 In mutual suspicion,
Wife thinks husband is cheating.
Husband believes wife is cheating.
Child thinks parent is lying.
Parent believes child is telling cock and bull.

The tax-collector believes the taxpayer is fibbing.
The taxpayer believes
The tax-collector is faking.
The politician thinks the electorate is fawning.
The electorate thinks
The politician is lying.

What a load of cock and bull!
Tired of hearing these phony tales?
Turn to ME!
I am the way, the truth, and the life.
Truthful lips endure forever,
But a lying tongue perishes forever.

FACES BEHIND MASKS

There's no question.
Our world is a stage
Where Tom, Dick, and Harry come to act,
Disguised behind multicolored masks,
Folks make believe in all walks of life!

This world is a stage
Foes act like friends,
Friends impersonate foes,
Mortals pass for immortals,
Humans think themselves superhuman.

This world is a stage
Miscreants act the pious,
Self-seekers masquerade as philanthropists,
Servants of Satan adorn the mask
Of holy men!

This globe is replete with impostors.
How long shall we dress in borrowed robes?
How much dust shall we throw into the eyes of friends?
How long shall we wear masks?
Tell me!

This world is truly a stage,
Like a masquerade dancing.
Hard to know whose story is real,
I call a spade a spade,
Couldn't care less whose ox is gored!

QUARANTINE

In bygone times,
It was heartening to see
Grandparents and grandchildren
Living under one roof,
Not anymore!

The gods of profit and
Egoism have decreed that
We put our golden-agers in makeshift homes,
Assisted-living homes where they are
Left to their own devices.
These hapless elderly persons
Languish in utter pathos.

Glued to wheelchairs;
Others bedridden;
Many more ravaged by dementia and Alzheimer's.

They bid time,
Waiting for the moment of call,
We've thrown our sense of
Duty to the dogs!
Shame on us!

RAT RACE

Time is pregnant with meaning--
Time and tide wait for no one,
A stitch in time saves nine,
Procrastination is the thief of time.
There's time for everything:

In bread-and-butter world,
Time is money--
Modus operandi for capital-mongers
Humanity and time are locked
In a vicious rat race headed for nowhere.

Folks can't eat anymore!
Folks can't rest anymore!
Folks can't play anymore!
Folks can't commune anymore!
Time's become an over-bearing master!

Homes are torn asunder,
Parents vie with one another for wealth.
Children left to their own devices have
The leeway to do to their heart's content.
I wonder when this infernal rat-race will stop.

WALLS

Jim Crow is dead
Long live Jim Crow!
Old habits die hard,
The requiem for Jim Crow
Was sung ages ago,
Yet Jim Crow lives on!

How many times
Have you been labeled misfit
For no other reason
But the color of your skin,
Shape of your nose
And texture of your hair?

How too often have you been subjected to
Less than dignified treatment
On account of the language you speak?
How often have they branded you bout d'homme[48]
You're less than human,
In coded terms?

How too often have you been
The target of veiled hate-speech?
How many times has the race card
Been used to shy away from giving
To Caesar what's Caesar's?
And to Lucifer what's Lucifer's?

Come to think of it,
Jim Crow isn't dead!
Hate-mongers and supremacists are Jim Crows!
Apartheid lovers are Jim Crows!
Jim isn't dead and buried,
He's merely built invisible walls around himself.

RAZZLE-DAZZLE

Our penchant for convoluted speech is notorious.
To make the inordinate seem ordinate,
Political intoxication has become political correctness.
To be a moron is to be intellectually challenged.
To be a drunk-driver is to drive under the influence.

Our love for obscure lingo is phenomenal.
Auto mechanics have known a re-rebirth,
They're automotive internists.
Elevator operators now pass for
Vertical transportation corps!

Our love for double-speak knows no bounds.
Pre-emptive counter-attack
Is a veil for our compulsive urge to wage war.
Tactical redeployment is the
Code-name for military retreat.

Our love for lexical ambivalence is incredible.
The Vietnam War dubbed
An incursion fails to
Qualify for an invasion.
We no longer talk of bullet holes

They're ballistic apertures
In the subcutaneous environment
Our neutron bombs have metamorphosed into
Radiation enhancement devices,
Such razzle-dazzle breeds fire-power.

FAMLA[49]

Concocted in heathen laboratories,
You pass off as African science.
You're the shame of humanity.
Your evil deeds legion,
Permeate all nooks and crannies.

Famla,
Decadent culture,
In your name, families are torn asunder
In your name, the young molest the elderly.
In your name, houses are burned down at random.

Famla,
In your name, kangaroo courts judge the innocent.
In your name, the law is flouted with impunity.
Witchcraft, you pit children against parents.
Because of you, sister rises against brother.

Famla
Because of you, cousin rises against cousin.
You're a stumbling block
To social harmony
It is time we kissed you farewell!

APOCALYPSE

Africa… Africa…Africa!
Africa fed colonialism
Africa fed capitalism
Africa fed imperialism
Africa now fed neo-colonialism.

In the beginning it was slavery,
Then it was colonization,
The ongoing neo-colonization is nefarious.
The euphoria of independence is no more.
Death has replaced life.

Despondency supplants hope
Indigence replaces opulence,
Internecine warfare steps in the shoes of fraternity.
Deconstruction supplants national construction,
Violence substitutes for peaceful coexistence.

Africa… Africa…Africa!
Water, water, water everywhere
But not a single drop to drink!
Her children feed on crumbs from the stranger's table.
Famine and malignancy their bedfellows

Land of abundance, land of scarcity!
Home to four horsemen of the apocalypse—
War, corruption, underdevelopment, disease.
Maimed, Mother Africa is caught
In a vicious cycle.

KAFFIR-BOY

Convoluted ego,
Monstrous bigotry,
Imbecilic idiocy,
Tearing people apart!
The tongue is fire,
The language a conflagration!

You call me Kaffir[50]-boy,
You brand me Bushman[51],
You say I'm a dirty Coolie[52],
But who are you, sanctimonious hypocrite?
Shame of humanity, you are!
Acme of tomfoolery.

Enter Eugène Ney Terre'Blanche[53],
Compulsive supremacist,
Backed by a cortege of Kaffir-haters
Their god is white,
And ours black like Satan.
Their creator must be a racist.

Fawning blasphemers!
Afrikaner Weerstandsbeweging (AWB),
Lucifer's fief on earth,
Its credo racial cleansing
Yet these dare-devils aren't masters of their tickling libido!
They fornicate with our sisters.

They rape our mothers,
The countless mulattoes
Teeming around are proof of their lascivious misdeeds,
Pathological liars!
Apartheid, the die is cast!
Your days numbered

Bow your head in shame,
We sang requiem for you in April 1994.
Nelson Mandela intoned the dirge,
And Frederick de Klerk echoed.
Apartheid, you belong in the trashcan of history,
Spent force you are. Adieu!

About the Author

Dr. Peter Wuteh Vakunta is a professor of African Languages and Literary Theory at the University of Wisconsin-Madison. He is novelist, poet, storyteller and essayist. Peter has published fifteen fictional and non-fictional works in the US, U.K. and Africa. These include *No Love Lost, Grassfields Stories from Cameroon, Lion Man and other Stories, Green Rape, Straddling the Mungo, Ntarikon, Mind Your P's and Q's, Nul n'a le monopole du français, Cry My Beloved Africa*, and more. His literary works have earned him prestigious prizes, not least of which is the Fay Goldie Award for excellence in creative writing. At present, Peter is working on a book on comparative literary studies, *Emerging Perspectives in the Francophone Novels of Africa and the Caribbean*.

NOTES

1 Leading a hand-to-mouth life
2 Mature women
3 Teenage girls
4 Times do not bode well
5 Things are topsy-turvy
6 The act of opening one's eyes, which means the "act of intimidating or making people fear"
7 It's slippery outside, which means the atmosphere is rife with uncertainty
8 No way!
9 Protest march in South Africa in the era of Apartheid
10 Cameroon
11 First president of Cameroon
12 Belief in a hand-to-mouth modus vivendi
13 Reference to Bate Besong's book of the same title.
14 Young children
15 Big shot
16 From the English word "care-taker". The word refers to a security guard in charge of a public place like a cinema, recreation ground, casino, etc. It entered Cameroon Pidgin English in the late 1980s among urban dwellers, as expressed essentially in oral discourse.
17 Children, speakers of Cameroon Pidgin English have used this word since 1980s.
18 Snail and by extension, a slow, nonchalant person .

19 Abbreviated from the word "mbutuku", which means "a good-for-nothing person, "weakling" or "idiot". Mainly used by young people, this loanword exists in Cameroon Pidgin English since the 1970s.

20 Reference to George Orwell book titled *1984* (1977)

21 Allusion to Tayo Olafioye's books of poems (2006)

22 Have sex with

23 Office messenger

24 Win

25 Lay off; fire

26 University of Yaoundé

27 Motor bike taxi

28 Policemen

29 Give a bribe

30 Allusion to the ruling party in Cameroon

31 Cameroonians

32 Hawkers

33 Market women

34 Wheel-cart pushers

35 Group of elderly women participating in a protest

36 Muslim from the north of Cameroon

37 Amulets

38 Female water spirits who from time to time haunt men

39 Rat

40 Witchcraft

41 Police officer in francophone Africa

42 Wheel-cart

43 Professor

44 Good bye

45 Mrs.

46 South African derogatory term for foreigner

47 Illegal immigrant

48 Less than human

49 Witchcraft

50 Derogatory name for black South African

51 Derogatory name of the Koi San
52 Derogatory name for South Africans of Asian origin
53 Leader of the white supremacist Afrikaner Resistance
   Movement (AWB) who was hacked and bludgeoned to
   death by two of his black farmhands in a dispute over wages
   on April 3, 2010